FLYING DINOSAURS

By Steven Lindblom
Illustrated by Christopher Santoro

Consultant: Lowell Dingus,
American Museum of Natural History

A GOLDEN BOOK • NEW YORK
Western Publishing Company, Inc., Racine, Wisconsin 53404

Final decisions concerning the content and illustrations for this book were made by the author and publisher.

Millions of years ago, when dinosaurs ruled Earth, pterosaurs (TARE-uh-sawrs) ruled the skies.

Most people think of these creatures as flying dinosaurs, but they were really only cousins of the dinosaurs. Pterosaurs and dinosaurs probably evolved from the same early reptiles, called thecodonts (THEEK-uh-donts).

The first pterosaur to be discovered and named
by scientists was Pterodactylus (tare-uh-DAK-til-us).
Pterodactylus was the size of a hawk and had a
long beak. It may have lived on the mud flats and
searched the mud at low tide for sea worms to eat.

Pterosaur means winged reptile. When the first pterosaur fossils were found 200 years ago, scientists thought pterosaurs must have been reptiles. Their heads and teeth were like those of alligators. But even though pterosaurs were reptiles, they must have looked very different from the reptiles that are living today.

All of today's reptiles are cold-blooded. A
cold-blooded creature can move quickly for only a
few minutes at a time. If it gets too cold, it moves
very slowly and must warm itself in the sun
before it can move quickly again. Since flying
would be hard for a cold-blooded animal, many
scientists now think pterosaurs were warm-
blooded like human beings.

Some pterosaurs were covered with fur! Once scientists decided that pterosaurs were reptiles, they assumed that the animals must have been covered with scaly reptile skin. But some people weren't so sure. They thought pterosaurs would have needed fur or feathers to keep them warm as they flew.

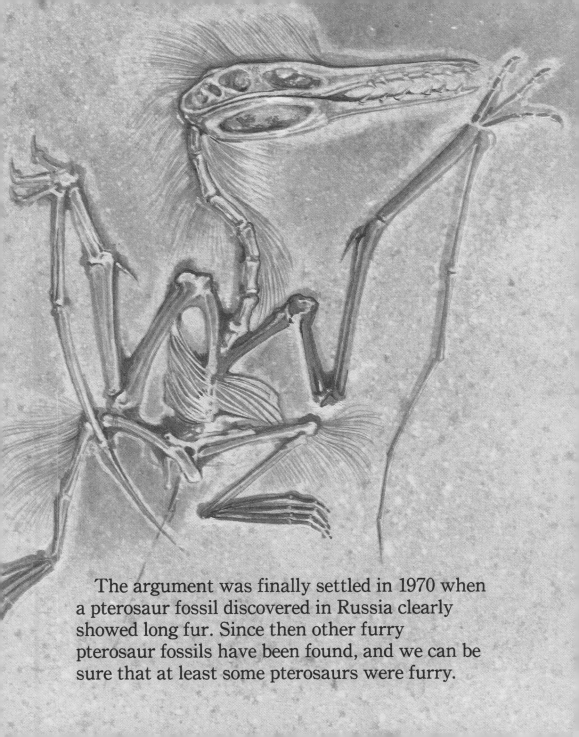

The argument was finally settled in 1970 when a pterosaur fossil discovered in Russia clearly showed long fur. Since then other furry pterosaur fossils have been found, and we can be sure that at least some pterosaurs were furry.

Everything we know about life in the age of
dinosaurs has been learned from studying fossils.
Fossils are made when a dead animal or plant
is buried in mud or sand. Over millions of years,
the mud turns to stone, leaving an imprint of the
plant or animal.

Studying fossils can tell us much about the pterosaurs. Fossil bones of smaller creatures inside a pterosaur fossil can tell us what pterosaurs ate. Fossils of plants and animals found nearby can tell us what the world was like when they lived. But there are some things we cannot learn from fossils. For example, we will never know for sure what color pterosaurs were.

We can make some pretty good guesses, though. Since pterosaurs lived like birds do today, they may have been colored like birds.

Their fur could have been colored for camouflage. The pterosaurs that lived by the sea may have been colored very much like today's seabirds—white underneath so the fish wouldn't see them against the sky, and a darker color on top so that larger pterosaurs wouldn't spot them from above.

Other pterosaurs that lived inland may have been brightly colored to blend in with the plants and trees. One, the Pterodaustro (tare-uh-DAWS-trow), probably lived in marshes like flamingos do today. It strained water through the bristles in its mouth to catch the tiny shrimp and algae the water contained. Since the flamingo gets its color from the shrimp it eats, some scientists wonder if the shrimp-eating Pterodaustro might have been a bright flamingo pink.

Pterosaurs came in all sizes. The smallest
known was the sparrow-sized Anurognathus
(an-ur-o-NAY-thus). It probably ate insects
like many tiny birds do today. The largest,
Quetzalcoatlus (ket-zahl-ko-AHT-los), may have
had wings that spread 75 feet wide—as wide a
wingspan as a twin-engined airplane!

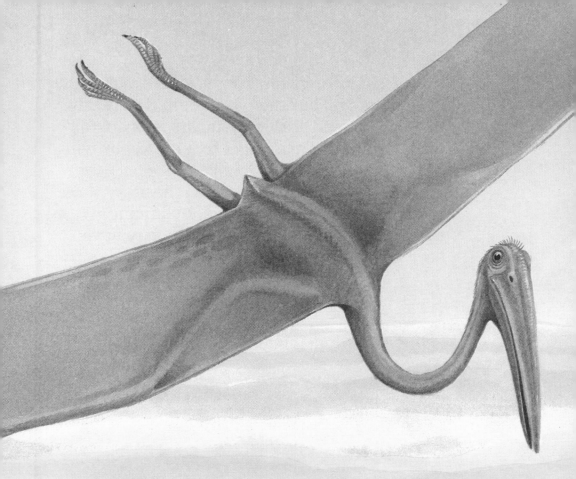

Pterosaur wings were made of tough skin
stretched between the body and the wing bones.
The bones in the wing were not all that different
from the ones in our own arms, except that one
finger was much longer than the others. It
was this finger that gave the pterodactyl
(tare-uh-DAK-til) its name, which means "wing
finger." The bones were hollow like a bird's to
make them light and strong.

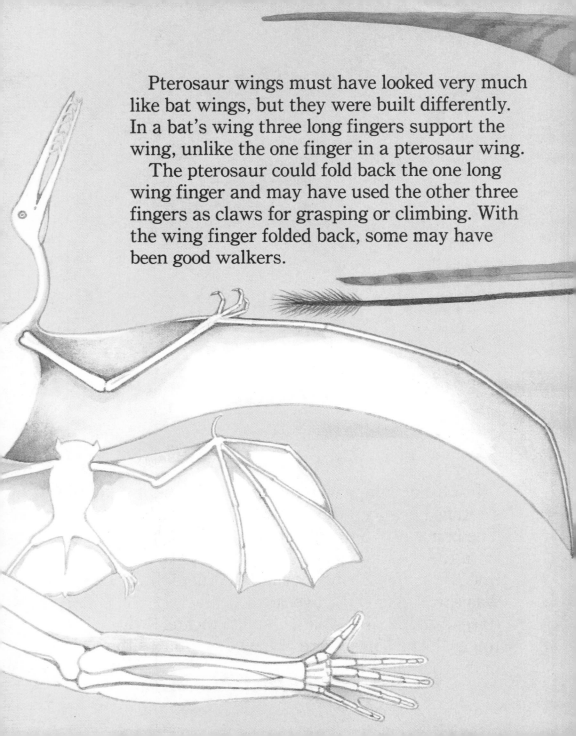

Pterosaur wings must have looked very much like bat wings, but they were built differently. In a bat's wing three long fingers support the wing, unlike the one finger in a pterosaur wing.

The pterosaur could fold back the one long wing finger and may have used the other three fingers as claws for grasping or climbing. With the wing finger folded back, some may have been good walkers.

When the pterodactyl was first discovered, it
looked so strange that some scientists did not
believe it could have flown. Some insisted it must
have been a swimmer, using its wings the way a
penguin does. Others thought it crept about
using its front arms as legs and feeding on dead
dinosaurs.

But now we are sure all pterosaurs could fly.
A group of scientists and engineers recently
managed to build a flying model of Quetzalcoatlus.
The structure of the arm bones proves once and
for all that Quetzalcoatlus could fly.

People often call any pterosaur a pterodactyl, but there were two kinds of pterosaurs: the rhamphorhynchids (ram-fo-RINK-ids) and pterodactylids (tare-uh-DAK-til-ids).

Rhamphorhynchids were the earliest pterosaurs. They were mostly small, and they had long tails that they must have used to steer and balance with while flying.

The little Rhamphorhynchus (ram-fo-RINK-us), from which all rhamphorhynchids get their name, had a diamond-shaped fin at the end of its long tail. It may have swooped down on fish and speared them with the long teeth that bristled from its mouth.

Another common rhamphorhynchid,
Dimorphodon (di-MOR-fo-don), had an enormous
head and a long tail. It may have lived in flocks
by the ocean, feeding on fish and squid.

Later pterosaurs had no tails. These are
called the pterodactylids, after Pterodactylus.
Pterodactylids had huge heads, often with
crests, which they may have used to steer with
while flying. They were the biggest and the last
of the pterosaurs.

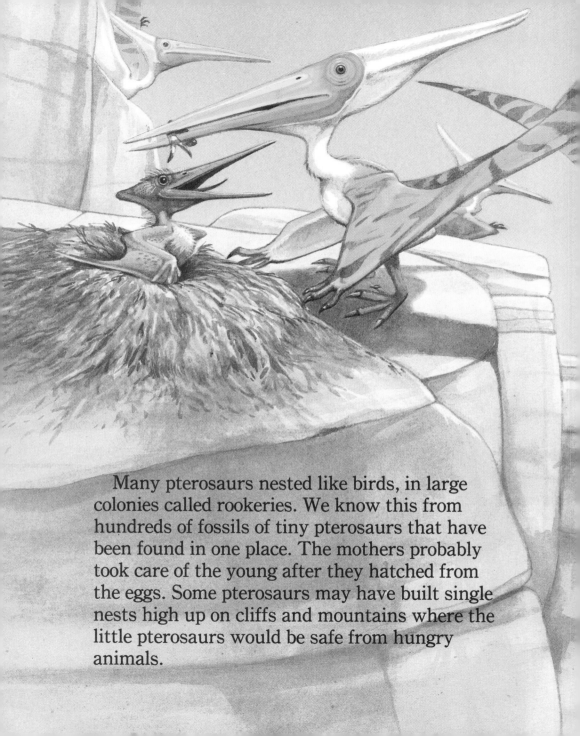

Many pterosaurs nested like birds, in large colonies called rookeries. We know this from hundreds of fossils of tiny pterosaurs that have been found in one place. The mothers probably took care of the young after they hatched from the eggs. Some pterosaurs may have built single nests high up on cliffs and mountains where the little pterosaurs would be safe from hungry animals.

Most pterosaurs that we know about lived near the seacoast, where they probably fished to eat and flew on steady sea breezes. The Pteranodon (tare-AN-uh-don) had a body about the size of a turkey and a head over six feet long! It needed a wingspan of 30 feet to get it into the air, and it was probably a very strong flier.

The largest pterosaur known, the gigantic Quetzalcoatlus, lived far inland. No one has yet found a complete skeleton of a Quetzalcoatlus, but we do know that it had a long neck and a toothless beak like a bird's.

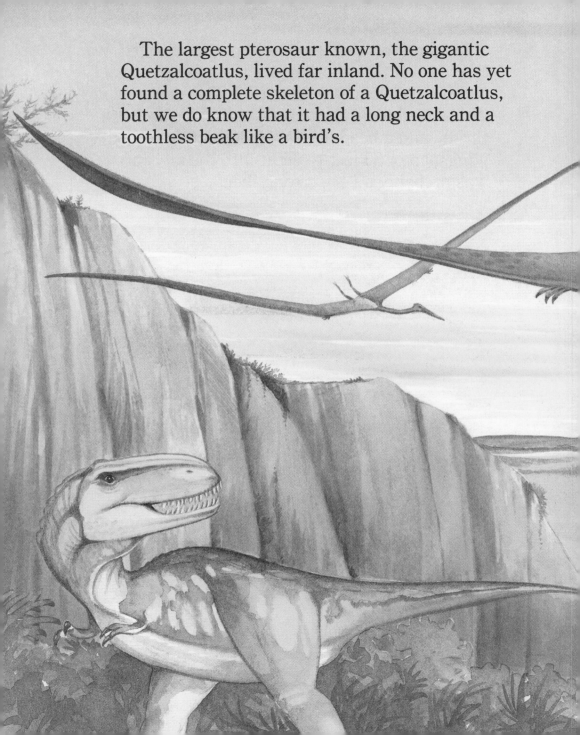

A big pterodactyl may not have been strong
enough to get airborne without help. Help could
come from the wind, or from a cliff from which to
leap. Once a pterodactyl was in the air, it would
soar like a hang glider, letting the air currents do
most of the work. Since a grounded pterosaur
would have been easy prey for a hungry
dinosaur, the larger pterodactyls would have
been very careful never to land when there
wasn't enough wind to take off again.

The great Quetzalcoatlus was not only the largest of the pterosaurs, it was the last of them. Sixty-five million years ago both pterosaurs and dinosaurs vanished from Earth. Scientists still cannot agree why. But imagine what it would be like to look up at the sky and see one of these pterosaurs soaring gracefully overhead!